T0194906

CROCODILE JERRY & PALS

ANTHONY "MARSMAN" BROWN

EDITOR : ARETHA BROWN

WestBow Press books may be ordered through booksellers or by contacting:

WestBow Press
A Division of Thomas Nelson & Zondervan
1663 Liberty Drive
Bloomington, IN 47403
www.westbowpress.com
1 (866) 928-1240

Because of the dynamic nature of the Internet, any web addresses or links contained in this book may have changed since publication and may no longer be valid. The views expressed in this work are solely those of the author and do not necessarily reflect the views of the publisher, and the publisher hereby disclaims any responsibility for them.

Any people depicted in stock imagery provided by Getty Images are models, and such images are being used for illustrative purposes only. Certain stock imagery © Getty Images.

ISBN: 978-1-9736-2628-2 (sc)
ISBN: 978-1-9736-2629-9 (e)

Library of Congress Control Number: 2018904774

Print information available on the last page.

WestBow Press rev. date: 04/20/2018

WESTBOW
PRESS®
A DIVISION OF THOMAS NELSON
& ZONDERVAN

CONTENTS

STORY 1
CROCODILE JERRY BECOMES A VEGETARIAN

Once upon a time there was a fearsome reptile by the name of Crocodile Jerry that lived in a lake. Fearing the wrath of God he wanted to change his ways from trying to eat people. He especially went after little boys who from time to time wanted to come and play in the lake, but because of Jerry's aggressiveness they could not.

In wanting to change his ways, Crocodile Jerry decided to became a vegetarian and because of that he wanted everyone to know and trust him. He knew he needed to work hard on becoming trustworthy because of his past actions and no one trusted him.

One day two young boys by the name of Joe and Paul who, once before had an encounter with Crocodile Jerry when he tried to eat them as they were walking on the road by the lake. Crocodile Jerry now wanting to be man's best friend saw them and shouted, "Hello there! Will you please be my friend?" The boys heard him shouting and when they looked around and saw Crocodile Jerry, they ran as fast as they could away from the road. No one knew that Crocodile Jerry had become a vegetarian and genuinely wanted to be their friend. Crocodile Jerry felt very sad and went below the water to hide his pain.

One afternoon when the boys, Joe and Paul were going home from school there was a sudden heavy downpour of rain which caused a lot of flooding on some roads. Because of the heavy flowing water, Joe and Paul tried to cross an old foot bridge which was their only route across the deep water on their way home. When they were in the middle of the bridge it gave way and they fell in the deep water which was flowing below. The water started washing them away and they shouted, "Help, help, help!" Things became very serious as no one could hear them because of the heavy downpour of rain. When the flowing water took them further down to the lake where Crocodile Jerry lived, they were still shouting for help but this time Crocodile Jerry heard them and came to their rescue. Crocodile Jerry swam up to them and told them to climb on his back, they were so desperate that they had to trust him this time and when they did that, Crocodile Jerry took them to safety. A warm thank you from the boys was given to Crocodile Jerry. It was the first time anyone had ever hugged him and the boys ran home to their parents feeling very relieved.

The next day when the rain subsided, the boys went to visit Crocodile Jerry by the lake, sat beside him and had their feet in the water. They became best of friends and everyone in the village was amazed by what they heard and started to trust Crocodile Jerry when he said he had become a vegetarian. They lived happily ever after.

THE END.

STORY 2
CROCODILE JERRY VS THE ALIENS FROM OUTER SPACE

One night while Crocodile Jerry was resting on the lake he saw a bright light coming down from the sky. He sat up and looked at it as it got closer and observed that it was a space ship from outer space. The space ship landed on the bank of the lake and about one hour after it landed the door of the ship opened and two strange looking creatures alighted from it.

When the space creatures saw Crocodile Jerry one of them said to the other, "If this is what the creatures on Earth looks like, it means that when ugliness was given away they got an overdose." Both of them laughed at the remark. The other creature replied, "I wouldn't want to see the ugliest!" Both of them laughed even more. Crocodile Jerry heard the corny joke that was cast in his direction and asked, "Excuse me! Who are you calling ugly?" The space creatures looked at each other in astonishment and replied together, "He talks too!" There was even more laughter.

The space creatures got serious and said to Crocodile Jerry, "We are here to conquer this planet and make everyone on it our slaves and we are going to start with you! If you were born on our planet we would bury you like a treasure because of your ridiculous look!" Crocodile Jerry told them to get the slave thought out of their minds because he will never be a slave for anyone. The space creatures gave Crocodile Jerry one hour to make up his mind and bow down to them or he would be sorry. Both of them went back in the space ship and closed the door.

After an hour had passed the space creatures came out of their ship again and saw Crocodile Jerry in a militant mood and asked him, "Well, have you made up your mind to be our slave?" At this moment, Crocodile Jerry said no words but was quietly inching closer to them, with none of them having the slightest idea how dangerous a crocodile can be when he was that close. The space creatures said, "If you will not consent we have no choice but to destroy you!" Both of them took out their weapons, laser guns, and fired at Crocodile Jerry hitting him in the back. To their surprise the weapons had no effect on Crocodile Jerry because the hide on his back was too thick so they looked at each other in amazement and fired again. This time when it failed and Crocodile Jerry snapped at them violently with his mouth, luckily for them they managed to jump out of the way with mere seconds to spare. One of the aliens even jumped so quickly one of the buttons on his pants was left in Crocodile Jerry's mouth. They ran back to the space ship with Crocodile Jerry in hot pursuit. They managed to close the door of the ship just in time to keep out Crocodile Jerry's attack. When the space creatures saw how close they came to be eaten by Crocodile Jerry they realized that planet Earth was no push over and it was best to leave quickly because they believe their weapons have no effect on Earth's creatures. They started the space ship engine and took off at terrific speed vowing never to return.

The next day Crocodile Jerry, the hero of the planet told his two friends Joe and Paul what had happened and they were thankful because if they were in Crocodile Jerry position the space creatures might have conquered the planet. They all lived happily ever after.

THE END.

STORY 3
CROCODILE JERRY CONFRONTING THE BULLIES

It was a nice sunny afternoon when Crocodile Jerry was relaxing on the bank of the lake taking in the sweet weather when he saw his two friends Joe and Paul running breathlessly towards him. When the boys got to Crocodile Jerry, he asked, "What's the matter why are you running like that?" The boys very exhausted took a while before they could catch their breath before they could answer. Paul who recovered quicker answered, "Ever since the new school year started and we went to a higher grade, some of the bigger boys have being chasing and bullying us. They even took away our lunch money and when we reported it to our teacher there was not enough proof to do anything because they denied everything!" "Is that so, well tomorrow we shall confront them," said Crocodile Jerry.

The next day when Joe and Paul were on their way to school they stopped by the lake and Crocodile Jerry told them of his plan. They agreed and went to school feeling very comfortable. When school was dismissed that evening, five of the notorious bullies waited for Joe and Paul determined that they wouldn't let them get away like yesterday. When Joe and Paul went through the school gate and saw them waiting, Joe and Paul ran according to the plan Crocodile Jerry had worked out. Joe and Paul ran past several blocks with the bullies in hot pursuit and when they reached the dead end alley that Crocodile Jerry said they should turn into, they did. The bullies were now thinking that they had Joe and Paul cornered in the alley, and started laughing and knocking their right fist into their left palm.

When the bullies started moving towards Joe and Paul to carry out their dirty plan they heard a loud clearing of throat behind them. When they looked behind them they saw the massive imposing structure of Crocodile Jerry standing with his knife and fork and a hungry look in his eyes. The bullies got terrified and started to plead with Crocodile Jerry not to eat them. Crocodile Jerry licking his lips looked at them and said, "I love noisy, naughty flesh and from the look of things you boys have been very naughty. Who should I start eating first?" "Not me, him!" Each of them said pointing at each other. "Well, I'm going to work out a deal with each of you. If you all promise to be good in the future then I might just change my mind about eating you now!" said Crocodile Jerry. "Yes, yes we will be good! As a matter of fact we'll be more than good!" The Bullies said. Crocodile Jerry looked at them, showed his large sharp teeth and said, "Go and always remember I'll be watching!" The bullies ran out of the alley in different direction all the way home never to bully anyone again. Joe, Paul and Crocodile Jerry went about their business and lived happily ever after.

THE END.

CROCODILE JERRY DETAINS THE BURGLAR

One evening Crocodile Jerry was on the bank of the lake relaxing when he saw a Police vehicle driving through the area with the sirens blaring. Crocodile Jerry being curious went down the road to his friend Joe's house to find out what was happening. In that district it was very unusual to see the Police busy. When Crocodile Jerry saw Joe and asked him what was happening, Joe told him that there were a lot of break ins into residents houses recently and nobody knew who the culprit was. The only available clue was the perpetrator's voice. Joe's aunt had heard it when he broke into her house down the block. She said when he was in the process of breaking in she started to shout "Thief!" and the thief boldly said while breaking in, "What, you calling me a thief? Wait till I come inside and you will know who is a thief!" The thief knew that nobody could hear her because of the distance she lived from everyone so he took advantage of that and had very easy access. So being alone all she could do was to lock herself in the bathroom while the thief cleared out the refrigerator and left.

Joe told Crocodile Jerry that all the break ins were done during the night when everyone retired to bed. When they awoke in the morning they would find their refrigerator empty. The only good thing about it was that the thief was only taking from the refrigerator even when they put a lock on it he would still manage to get in. Everyone in the district was now living on the edge because they were not feeling safe anymore and they didn't want to start suspecting or accusing anyone without proof. So Crocodile Jerry worked out a plan with Joe because they were determined to put an end to the thief's reign of terror.

The following night Crocodile Jerry and Joe locked themselves into Joe's house, turned off all the lights, and left the window to the road wide open with the refrigerator in sight to lure the thief inside. They would lie in wait for about two hours until they saw someone outside shining a light into the house, trying to see if anyone was inside. It was the thief and when he was satisfied and thinking that the coast was clear he smiled and said to himself, "Well, they finally learned that I'm unstoppable." He climbed in through the open window and easily entered the house.

When the thief put his big bag on the ground and opened the refrigerator to unload its contents, Crocodile Jerry who was not seen by the thief lying flat on his belly in the dark opened his mouth and grabbed on to the thief's leg. While Crocodile Jerry was holding him, Joe turned on the lights in the house and called the police. While the Police were on their way the thief begged Crocodile Jerry not to eat him. The way he was begging you couldn't believe it was the same bold person who threatened Joe's aunt a few days ago.

When the Police arrived and put the thief in handcuffs, the thief said "I never knew I would live to see the day that I would be glad to see the police." He thanked the Police for rescuing him from becoming Crocodile Jerry's meal and vowed never to come back after his sentence is finished. Everyone in the district thanked Crocodile Jerry and they felt safe again and lived happily ever after.

THE END.

STORY 5
CROCODILE JERRY
AT HALLOWEEN

It was fast approaching the Halloween season and everyone in town was getting their Halloween costumes ready for the annual Halloween party. Joe and Paul went to visit Crocodile Jerry by the lake to tell him about the party and about their costumes. Crocodile Jerry was thrilled to hear and wanted to go with them to the planned party. When Crocodile Jerry asked them if he could come, the boys hesitated for a while because not everyone at the party would be from the district and that could be a big scare. When Crocodile Jerry saw that the boys hesitated to give an answer he became very sad because they were his best friends. Right away Paul came up with an idea and said, "Everyone at the party will be dressed in costumes so if you come as you are they won't know if you are wearing a costume or not but one thing though we are going to have to get you a pair of shoes." Crocodile Jerry was very relieved when he heard that and immediately started looking forward to the party.

The day before the party Joe and Paul took Crocodile Jerry to the shoes store to get him a pair of shoes. When Crocodile Jerry tried on several pairs of shoes ranging from size ten to fourteen they all felt tight so Joe suggested that Crocodile Jerry should go around the back and wash his feet and come back. Crocodile Jerry went and did just that and when he returned and tried on some more pairs, surprisingly a size six was his best fit. All three of them were now relieved that they got the right fit and went home.

The night of the party the three of them travelled together with Joe dressed like a bat, Paul dressed like an elephant and Crocodile Jerry in his birth suit with every one thinking that he had on a costume. Crocodile Jerry had an encounter with a baby boy while his mother was holding him up in her arms. The baby boy kept stretching across and grabbing onto Crocodile Jerry face saying, "Mommy, mommy I want this mask!" The boy's mother politely apologized to Crocodile Jerry not knowing herself that he was real. Apart from Joe and Paul only a cat knew that Crocodile Jerry was real, he used his cat instinct and sensed that going near to Crocodile Jerry was very dangerous so he ran out of the party never to come back.

The DJ changed the pace of the music and started playing the crowd's favorite music which was Reggae Music. Everyone took to the dance floor including Crocodile Jerry and started to shake their legs but the spotlight was mostly on Crocodile Jerry doing the crocodile skank. Everybody on the dance floor started following Crocodile Jerry and trying to learn the new dance that was catchy and seen for the first time. Crocodile Jerry became a star and after the party everyone went home vowing to master the new dance they learned and lived happily after.

THE END.

STORY 6
CROCODILE JERRY IN THE DONUT CONTEST

*O*ne evening Joe, Paul and Crocodile Jerry were sitting by the lake when they heard a vehicle with a loud speaker driving pass the lake. They were advertising a donut eating contest to be held in the district on the weekend and the winner of the contest will receive two bicycles to be shared between himself and his best friend. When the vehicle stopped Joe went up and collected two forms for himself and Paul, which was to be filled out and handed in if they were interested in entering the contest.

The next day Joe and Paul were discussing the contest with Crocodile Jerry because they discovered that each contestant will have to eat one hundred large donuts in order to win. They thought the rules of the contest were unfair because nobody can eat one hundred large donuts in one day. They also discovered that this contest was held all across the country and nobody was ever able to win it, even the most gluttonous individuals have tried and couldn't do it.

Right away Crocodile Jerry after hearing everything came up with an idea. He said that he found a magic lamp once and when he rubbed it a genie came out and offered him a wish to change him into a human being for a day. Crocodile Jerry said he didn't bother with it because if he took up the offer he would change back to a crocodile in twenty-four hours so he just ignored it and buried the lamp at the bottom of the lake. Crocodile Jerry's plan was to now enter the contest then find the lamp and take the genie's offer of turning him into a human being on the contest day. With his huge appetite Crocodile Jerry was determined to win the bicycles for his two friends Joe and Paul.

On the contest day Crocodile Jerry dug up the lamp, rubbed it and the genie appeared and changed him into a human being. He got dressed with the clothes Joe brought for him and went to the place of the contest along with Joe and Paul. But when they reached they discovered that Crocodile Jerry now looking human was the only contestant. The people putting on the contest looked at Crocodile Jerry and said, "Why are you wasting your time? Nobody can eat one hundred large donuts in a day! But since you're so brave we are going to put you to the test!" They prepared a table with one hundred fresh donuts, laughed and said, "Let's see how good you are, you may begin choking yourself!"

When Crocodile Jerry started eating the donuts everyone present looked on in amazement because of the speed he was eating the donuts and in a short space of time all one hundred donuts were in his stomach. Crocodile Jerry gave off a loud belch which could be heard a mile away and was greeted with a thunderous applause from everyone who attended. Crocodile Jerry was given his prize of two bicycles which he immediately handed to his best friends Joe and Paul who rode them home.

At the twenty fourth hour after the wish was granted, Crocodile Jerry changed back to his usual self and they all lived happily ever after.

THE END.

STORY 7
CROCODILE JERRY WARNS THE PITBULL

One evening after school Joe and Paul rode their bicycles down to the lake to visit their friend Crocodile Jerry. After sitting and talking for a while they told Crocodile Jerry goodbye because they had to visit Joe's aunt, who had invited them over for their favorite pie.

As they were leaving, Crocodile Jerry saw that they were heading in a different direction and asked them, "I thought the way to your aunt was that way?" Because Crocodile Jerry went there before and knew the shortest direction he was wandering if they had forgotten the way. Paul answered, "Yes that's the shortest route but because of Zull the fierce Pitbull, we would rather travel the longer route." "What fierce Pitbull are you talking about?" asked Crocodile Jerry. The boys started to explain to Crocodile Jerry that last month a house on the way to his aunt was sold to a man who had a mean Pitbull and to date the dog had chased and tried to bite anyone who walked or rode past the house. "Is that so?" said Crocodile Jerry, who had dealt with several situations like that before.

Because of what Crocodile Jerry had just heard he decided to travel with his friends taking the shortest route to their aunt's just to see what this mean Zull looked like. When they were approaching the yard, Zull came out and stood in their way and said, "The only beast that can pass my territory for free and get maximum respect is the lion which is king and all conquering. Everyone else must pay their way with ten cans of dog food, so if you don't have that turn back now before it's too late!" Zull's owner who was standing there also said, "I will not be held responsible for anyone who steps out of line and gets bitten so please obey orders!"

Joe and Paul stood behind Crocodile Jerry that just stood there looking and licking his lips not saying a word. Obviously Zull had never seen a crocodile in his entire life or knew what the crocodile was capable of. Crocodile Jerry spoke for the first time and very politely said to Zull, "Can we have a beast to beast talk in private please?" Zull said, "You better be quick because I'm getting very hungry and running out of patience!" When Crocodile Jerry and Zull went to the side of the road in private Crocodile Jerry whispered something in his ears. Zull after hearing what Crocodile Jerry had whispered opened his eyes wide looked at his large sharp teeth and said, "For real!" Zull started to tremble and with a terrified look turned around with his tail tucked between his hind legs, and ran off with terrific speed. He ran so fast he ran past his own yard screaming all the way. Zull's owner who witnessed what happened asked Crocodile Jerry, "What have you done to my dog? What did you say to him that caused him to behave like that?" Crocodile Jerry replied, "All I said was the last time I saw a lion I had him for dinner and he will be my supper this evening if he doesn't get out of the way and be nice." Zull's owner also stepped aside.

The next day when Joe and Paul rode pass Zull's house on their way to visit their aunt, Zull and his owner could be seen peeking at them through the window of the house and never caused any more problems again. Everyone lived happily ever after.

THE END.

STORY 8
CROCODILE JERRY
VS THE DEER

It was a warm sunny day when Crocodile Jerry was lying on the bank of the lake enjoying the mid-day sun when he was approached by Keke, the Deer who had a curious look on his face. "Good day to you Mr. Crocodile Jerry," said Keke. "Good day to you also Keke but what have I done so marvelous that I should get such an unexpected visit from one that looks so tasty and eloquent?" asked Crocodile Jerry with a smile on his face. Even though Keke was having this conversation with Crocodile Jerry he was very alert and watchful while standing sharply on his toes because no deer in the world trust a crocodile even when he says he had become a vegetarian.

The conversation continued with Keke saying to Crocodile Jerry, "I am here to set the record straight. Animal researchers are spreading a terrible rumor that the crocodile is faster than the deer over a short distance of about twenty to thirty yards." "Is that so? I wasn't aware of that," replied a smiling Crocodile Jerry. "How on earth did animal researchers come by that rumor? Only God knows. So I am challenging you Crocodile Jerry to a short distance race which will put an end to that rumor." said Keke. "What is the prize?" asked Crocodile Jerry. "A prize is not necessary because I don't need one and you definitely have no chance against my four tall legs when all you do is swim around in water and crawl on your belly most of the time." said Keke.

The date of the race was set and Joe, Paul and all the creatures that lived nearby were invited as witnesses. The only concern for some was thinking the impossible could happen and Crocodile Jerry wins. Keke during the days leading up to the race was so confident that the impossible thought didn't even come to mind. But it was Tobi the Snake that warned Keke that his ancestors in Africa were always aware of the sudden burst of speed of the crocodile and Crocodile Jerry was looking too confident.

On the day of the race the distance of thirty yards was carefully measured and marked by Joe with a photo finish camera set up at the finish line, in case the impossible should happen. The two runners Crocodile Jerry and Keke were called to the starting blocks by Paul, the race starter. Then they were asked to get down on their marks, set with Crocodile Jerry getting up off his belly and going high on his toes. When Paul fired the starter gun both were off in a flash and were neck and neck the entire way until they hit the finish line. To the surprise of every one who witnessed, it looked like a dead heat but when the camera was checked Crocodile Jerry with his long nose hit the finish line first.

Keke couldn't believe the speed of Crocodile Jerry but when he saw the photo finish picture he held down his head and conceded defeat. Keke headed back to the woods knowing now that all deer must keep their distances from a crocodile because they are not as sluggish as their looks. The message from this is never to under estimate your opponent in any competition and the speed of Crocodile Jerry is still spoken about today.

THE END.

STORY 9
CROCODILE JERRY
SAVES THE LAKE

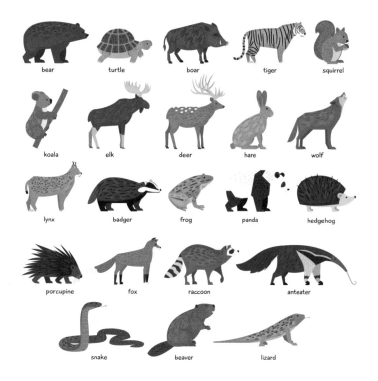

bear · turtle · boar · tiger · squirrel

koala · elk · deer · hare · wolf

lynx · badger · frog · panda · hedgehog

porcupine · fox · raccoon · anteater

snake · beaver · lizard

It was a cool windy night when Crocodile Jerry and his water friend Bobo the Turtle were relaxing in the lake. The sun had just set and the full moon was lighting up the night with all its glory when they saw a truck marked "Waste Water" on the side backing up to the lake. Crocodile Jerry and Bobo, seeing the strange truck backing up to the lake started watching it carefully to see what whoever was driving it was up to. The truck also had a foul smell.

The truck stopped at the edge of the lake and a man got out and pulled out a large hose. He was about to empty the contents of the truck in the lake when Crocodile Jerry shouted to him, "Hold it right there Mister, what you're about to do is not allowed!" The man not sure who was shouting to him in the dark replied, "Everything in this truck will be emptied here tonight and it's none of your business!" "Is that so, well let me tell you something, all the creatures in the woods depend on this lake for survival so we can't allow you to do that!" "Then who is going to stop me?" asked the man who was determined to carry out his act.

All the creatures in the woods were now alerted to what was taking place and Dundo the Hedgehog used his sharp pointed spikes to puncture the wheels of the truck which made the driver of the truck panic when he heard the hissing as the air left the tires. "What do you want?" asked the truck driver who is now realizing that the creatures he couldn't see in the dark meant serious business.

Crocodile Jerry walked up behind the truck driver in the dark and said, "Hello sir, you must now consider yourself the luckiest man in the world, we warned you but you would not listen now you and this truck are going to stay here until the Police arrives." The truck driver turned around and saw the massive imposing structure of Crocodile Jerry and became terrified and started to beg, "Please don't eat me I'll do anything, I'm so sorry!" "I will not waste my time eating you," replied Crocodile Jerry.

While all this was taking place Paku the Owl flew up to Joe's house and told him what was happening. Joe telephoned the Police and ran down to the lake as the Police made their way. The situation by the lake before the Police arrived was very tense because all the creatures had gotten into a militant mood and Crocodile Jerry was trying to hold them off the truck driver.

When Joe and the Police arrived on the scene the Police arrested the truck driver and said, "This is not the first time something like this has taken place but this is the first time we are catching somebody red handed. The judge in court is going to look very serious at this." The Police read the truck driver his rights before taking him away in handcuffs. A tow truck was sent by the Police to remove the truck later. All the creatures rejoiced and lived happily ever after when they saw the truck driver leaving in the back of the Police vehicle.

THE END.

STORY 10
CROCODILE JERRY VS THE POACHERS

*O*ne night Crocodile Jerry had a dream that a mighty angel from God appeared to him and told him that he was pleased with the progress he had made in becoming a vegetarian. The angel also told Crocodile Jerry that he must be very careful because two poachers will be coming to the lake looking for him and their intentions are not good, therefore he must be prepared.

The next day when Crocodile Jerry saw his two friends Joe and Paul, he told them about the dream and told them if they saw any strangers in the district they should tell him. Joe and Paul left and went into town and started to ask their friends in town if they had seen any strange men. When they asked the newspaper vendor he told them, "Yes, two strange men just stopped and bought a newspaper and I overheard them saying they are going to the bar to have a drink." Joe and Paul went into the bar and saw the two strangers and sat in the seat behind them where they could hear their conversation. One of the strangers kept hinting to the other that they are going to be rich tonight because the size of that crocodile will make many top of the line hand bags and shoes. Joe looked at Paul with his eyes wide open and said, "These are definitely the two men Crocodile Jerry dreamt about and their plan seems to be targeting Crocodile Jerry tonight. Let's go tell Crocodile Jerry so he can be prepared!"

When Joe and Paul ran back to the lake and told Crocodile Jerry what they heard the strangers saying, immediately Crocodile Jerry started making preparations. Crocodile Jerry dug a large deep hole at the front of the lake and covered it with bushes.

When the sun set and it got dark Crocodile Jerry, Joe and Paul lie in wait for the poachers to arrive. About an hour later they heard footsteps and saw lights coming in their direction when Crocodile Jerry shouted to them, "Go back where you came from because poaching is illegal!" The poachers with their rifles in hand replied, "We are here for you and we are not going to leave without you because you and all the crocodiles in this region are going to make us rich! So it's best if you surrender now because we are too mean to oppose!" "Come and get me I'm over here!" replied Crocodile Jerry. The poachers started running confidently towards the sound of the voice when suddenly there was a loud crash. The poachers fell into the trap that was set and could not get out because the hole was too deep. Crocodile Jerry sent Joe and Paul to call the Police while he stood guard till the Police arrive. "I warned you but you did not listen now you're going to pay the price!" said Crocodile Jerry to the poachers in the hole who begged for a chance.

When the police arrived and saw the men the sergeant said, "These men are wanted for poaching and it seems as if they have met their match, good work!" The poachers were taken away in handcuffs by the Police and they won't be free for a very long time. Everyone in the district was relieved and they lived happily ever after.

THE END.

Printed in the United States
By Bookmasters